To Dany, Gary and Charlene who supported
me during the realisation of this book.

To Maria, Anne-Louise and Dee, who believed in me.

And to Barnaby, who found me and
became the love of my life –
thank you.

First published 2014 by Walker Books Ltd

87 Vauxhall Walk, London SE11 5HJ

2 4 6 8 10 9 7 5 3 1   © 2014 Valentina Mendicino

The right of Valentina Mendicino to be identified as author/illustrator
of this work has been asserted by her in accordance with the
Copyright, Designs and Patents Act 1988

This book has been typeset in ITC Cheltenham

Printed in China

British Library Cataloguing in Publication Data: a catalogue
record for this book is available from the British Library

ISBN 978-1-4063-5584-0   www.walker.co.uk

The Really Abominable Snowman

Valentina Mendicino

WALKER BOOKS
AND SUBSIDIARIES
LONDON · BOSTON · SYDNEY · AUCKLAND

In a deep, dark cave,
high in the Himalayas,
there lived ... a creature.

It was said that he was huge, horrible and VERY hairy ...

that he ATE lost children ...

and that he smelt like old cheese.

Ew!

He was terrifying!

He was **hideous**!

He WAS ...

The Really Abominable Snowman!

Or Milo, as his mum called him.

And, actually, Milo was not at all hideous. Of course he didn't eat CHILDREN!

He ate cherry cupcakes! (Lots of them.)

Milo really enjoyed craft time.

And he was very neat, too. He kept his cave spotless

and scrubbed himself
every day with lavender soap.

But it didn't matter.

To everyone else,
he was simply ...

No-one knew who the real Milo was.
He hated it when people ran away from him.

Milo only wanted a friend,
a friend to share his cupcakes with.

**Milo just didn't understand what
he was doing wrong.**

A MAKE

TOO STREET.

Too rock.

TOO POSH.

Too punk.

OVER!

TOO HIPPIE.

Too French.

Too Gaga!

EEK! NO! TOO MUCH.

Then Milo heard that "social networks"
were a great way to make friends.
So he decided to have a go.

First, he tried to send
out a "tweet".

But maybe he was a little too ... loud.

So he tried again.
Milo was one determined Yeti!

But he still didn't find any new friends.
Maybe he was looking in the wrong "book"...

Until one day, Milo spotted a notice in the *Himalayan Times...*

MISUNDERSTOOD HIM. It was just no use, Milo would always be a *Really Abominable Snowman.*

Milo felt so lonely.

But then...

Milo had a friend. And guess what?
Sophie (as her mum called her)
loved cupcakes, too!

Something happened. **Something very special.**

And Milo knew that there will always be someone who loves you, no matter what you are.